AVERY'S GIFT

WRITTEN BY
JONATHAN HOEFER

ILLUSTRATED BY
MILANA SAMARSKAYA

4

In the darkness of the summer night,
Avery opened her curious eyes.
Her bedroom looked familiar,
but it felt a different size.

Her curtains seemed to flow and dance,
partnered by the air.
Garden crickets beeped and chirped
inviting her out there.

She sat up slowly in her bed
with the moonlight on her face
and looked around her darkened room—
but things were out of place.

Her furniture was different,
yet the wallpaper looked the same.
The flowers stared and winked at her...
for tonight, they played a game.

The flowers started to swirl around.
From the wall, their stems broke free.
One smiling rose came close to Avery
and whispered, "Come with me!"

She stepped right out of her comfy bed
and felt the coolness of the floor.
She allowed the flower to take her hand
and lead her toward the door.

The color of her skin seemed pale,
her nightgown, a pinkish-white.
"Where did all of my colors go?
Are they hiding in the night?"

The evening creatures welcomed Avery—
some fireflies, first to arrive.
A halo formed above her head...
and the garden came alive!

She danced right through a field of flowers
with hues of lavender and blue.
"But where have all MY colors gone?"
She didn't have a clue.

But the buzzing of the night continued;
the moon just beamed with pride.
As butterflies delivered Avery kisses,
a fox slinked by her side.

"Oh, hello, Mr. Fox! I've lost my colors.
Can you help me find them, please?"
The fox then gave her a wink and a nod
and carried her through the trees.

The two new friends followed a path
that led to a pebble beach shore.
And even though this place was new,
she felt she had been there before.

The pebbles glistened by the light of the moon
as the sapphire waves were lapping.
The helpful fox took her toward a tree
where a wise, old owl was napping.

"Excuse me, Owl," asked Avery.
"Do you know where my colors might be?"
The sleepy owl slowly opened his eyes
and pointed toward the sea.

From the misty fog on the water,
a boat then came into view.
The smiling boy on board was waving,
so Avery waved back, too.

The boat was detailed and brightly colored—
his outfit was just the same.
Through the rolling clouds a voice was heard,
"Hello, there! What's your name?"

"I'm Avery," she responded proudly.
"I'm Dalton," he said in return.
"I'm not exactly sure where I am.
 I feel I have a lot to learn."

The owl then flew from his cozy perch
and landed on the oar.
Dalton smiled and glanced at the bird
as his boat then came to shore.

"You live here, then?" asked Dalton.
"What a beautiful place to be."
Avery replied: "I think I do.
But, things seem odd to me.

"You see, when I woke up in my bed tonight,
a rose took me right from my covers.
But the most confusing thing for me
is that I seem to have lost my colors."

"Let's find them together!" said Dalton.
"I have faith in us that we can!"
So quickly up the limestone path,
the fox and the children ran.

They jogged up hills and walked on logs
and frolicked through meadows serene.
They played endless rounds of hopscotch
under willows vibrant and green.

Dalton told stories of adventure
as Avery sang songs about flowers.
They shared silly stories and played funny games
that seemed to last for hours.

Laughing, they raced through the open fields
and danced beneath a tree.
They shared their thoughts about the universe
and worlds they couldn't see.

"I'm sorry we didn't find your colors.
They will come to you some day."
Sadly, he glanced at the rising moon—
he had to be on his way.

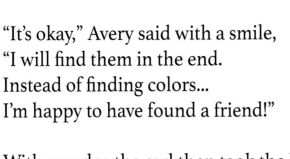

"It's okay," Avery said with a smile,
"I will find them in the end.
Instead of finding colors...
I'm happy to have found a friend!"

With a nudge the owl then took the kids
to the patiently waiting boat.
Avery and Dalton paused on the shore.
She did not want him to go.

Dalton pointed across the water,
"Hear that music over the sea?
I have been given a map and an invitation—
people are waiting there for me."

Dalton then turned slowly to Avery.
"I have a gift for you.
It is an item very valuable to me,
but it is something I must do."

Avery's eyes grew wide with tears
as Dalton reached into his pocket.
The nighttime stars illuminated the gift.
It was a beautiful, heart-shaped locket.

"No, no, I can't. It should stay with you."
But Dalton knew it was best.
He placed the chain around her neck
and the locket upon her chest.

Avery's cheeks then flourished and glowed
as the tears ran down her face.
"We are soul friends now, forever," he said,
giving her a warm embrace.

With this honest hug came energy and love
that she felt from head to toe,
as Dalton witnessed her colors come back
to her face, her lips, her clothes.

"Oh, this has been such a magical night!
But, it is time for me to leave."
Avery gave Dalton her thanks once more.
It was all too much to believe.

The majestic owl guided Dalton away
in his boat, where the horizon ends.
As Avery shouted from the pebbled shore,
"We are now forever friends!"

Avery turned and clenched the locket
and ran toward home so swift
as she felt the power of her newfound colors
that came from Dalton's gift.

The End

The True Story of Avery and Dalton

Dalton Lawyer was born on January 17, 2001. He was a vibrant, active boy with a contagious laugh and sparkling personality. Dalton's energy and passion for life lit up a room and all those who knew him. He was a big brother and idolized by his three younger triplet siblings—Tai, Miles, and Austin—and he was the true North for his loving parents, Jeri and Jim. Commanding attention where ever he went, Dalton was cherished for his youthful, yet strikingly handsome features coupled with his vivacious spirit and determination in life.

Avery Toole was born on April 21, 2004. Despite her beautiful, robust, and spunky temperament, hours after she was born, it was discovered that Avery had a very complex congenital heart defect known as HLHS. Avery underwent her first open heart surgery at five days old, and over the next several years, had an additional eight open heart surgeries, four cardiac arrests, and was ultimately placed on a mechanical heart pump at age five for terminal heart failure. Avery lived her life unable to run and play or even walk up several stairs without being breathless and blue. She experienced life from the sidelines, often sitting alone at playdates or birthday parties watching other children do what she was unable to because of her failing heart.

The lives of these two children 800 miles apart—unlikely to ever intersect.

On August 5, 2009, eight-year-old Dalton Lawyer lost his life suddenly and tragically in a biking accident. His parents, Jeri and Jim—a nurse and an anesthesiologist—during their darkest moment and inexplicable grief, made the decision to donate Dalton's organs. Dalton saved four individuals through his gift of life.

On August 6, 2009, Avery received his heart.

Avery lives with her parents, Cheryl and Mike, in Hopkinton, Massachusetts. She is a healthy, vibrant young girl with a sparkling personality whose vivacious spirit and passion for life lights up a room and the lives of all who know her.

A Message *from the* Toole *and* Lawyer Families

We would like to acknowledge and extend our deepest gratitude to families who are placed in the inexplicable circumstance of making end-of-life decisions considering organ donation. Without your selfless generosity, stories like Avery's and Dalton's would never exist.

In addition, we would like to thank the medical professionals who make organ transplantation possible. The courage they possess to have meaningful conversations with families navigating end-of-life decisions and the orchestration of the countless teams necessary to transplant the gift of life from donor to recipient is life-changing for all. Their tireless work, dedication, and special care are truly invaluable.

Register *to be a* Donor!

Register to be an organ, eye, and tissue donor through Donate Life America.

Donate Life America works to increase the number of donated organs, eyes, and tissues available to save and heal lives through transplantation. More than 100,000 men, women, and children are waiting for lifesaving organ transplants.

You can help by registering to be an organ, eye, and tissue donor at **RegisterMe.org/Averys_Gift**

Register today to be an organ, eye & tissue donor.
RegisterMe.org